This book is to be returned before
the l[...]

D1436018

For Marsha Dixon

The rights of Ruth Brown to be identified as the author and illustrator of this work have been asserted by her in accordance with the Copyright, Designs and Patents Act, 1988.

First published in Great Britain in 1994 by Andersen Press Ltd., 20 Vauxhall Bridge Road, London SW1V 2SA. Published in Australia by Random House Australia Pty., 20 Alfred Street, Milsons Point, Sydney, NSW 2061. All rights reserved. Colour separated in Switzerland by Photolitho AG, Offsetreproduktionen, Gossau, Zürich. Printed and bound in Italy by Grafiche AZ, Verona.

10 9 8 7 6 5 4 3 2 1

British Library Cataloguing in Publication Data available.

ISBN 0 86264 462 3

This book has been printed on acid-free paper

COPYCAT
RUTH BROWN

Ⓐ
Andersen Press · London

There was once a black cat called Holly. She was the mother of Baby and Buddy and they all lived with Bessie the dog. Baby was shy and kept to herself but Buddy was the opposite. Buddy was a copycat.

Holly liked to daydream by
the window – so did Buddy.

When Holly sat by the fire
warming her back, Buddy
warmed his feet, unless

Baby liked to sleep on the
window seat – so did Buddy.

He even copied the squirrels,

and the birds,

Bessie was
chewing a bone and Buddy
decided that what was right for
Bessie was right for Copycat.

But Buddy was wrong.

Cats' teeth aren't made for
chewing bones, and,

Even though his tongue
hangs out now, Buddy
hasn't changed a bit.

He's still the same
old Copycat.